© Disney

© Disney

© Disney

© Disney

© Disney

© Disney

D1531189

Press-out pencil toppers

Push the end of your pencil up through the bottom slit and back through the top slit to secure each pencil topper in place.

Disney
M⊚ANA
Born to Voyage

MOANA1190583

Code is valid for your Moana ebook and may be
redeemed through the Disney Story Central app on the App Store.
Content subject to availability. Parent permission required.
Code expires on December 31, 2019.

PaRragon

Bath · New York · Cologne · Melbourne · Delhi
Hong Kong · Shenzhen · Singapore

Seashell Search

Baby Moana finds a shell on the seashore.
How many shells can you count on this page?

Great counting!

Add a reward
sticker here.

I can count ___ shells

Answer on page 31

Turtle Rescue

Little Moana meets a baby turtle on the beach.
Which path should the turtle take to reach the ocean?

a

b

c

Did you find it?

Add a reward
sticker here.

3

Answer on page 31

First Mates

Cute little Pua is saying hello to his
friend Heihei, the silly rooster!
Copy the colors to complete the picture below.

Great coloring!

Add a reward
sticker here.

Island Chief

Tui is the ruler of Monunui, but he's also Moana's dad!
How many times can you find 'TUI' in the grid below?
Look up, down, forward, and backward.

T	U	I	U	T
A	V	R	A	H
I	C	T	A	G
U	I	U	T	A
T	A	L	J	Q

'TUI' appears

☐

times.

Super searching!

Add a reward sticker here.

Answers on page 31

Sailing Spirit

Adventurous Moana has always dreamed of exploring the ocean. Design a brand new sail for her boat.

Cool drawing!

Add a reward sticker here.

Hero of Oceania

Maui is a mythical warrior with a magical fishhook.
Copy this picture into the grid below, square by square.

That looks great!

Add a reward sticker here.

Find Your Way

Can you guide these boats safely through the reef?
Trace along each path with a pencil,
without touching the sides.

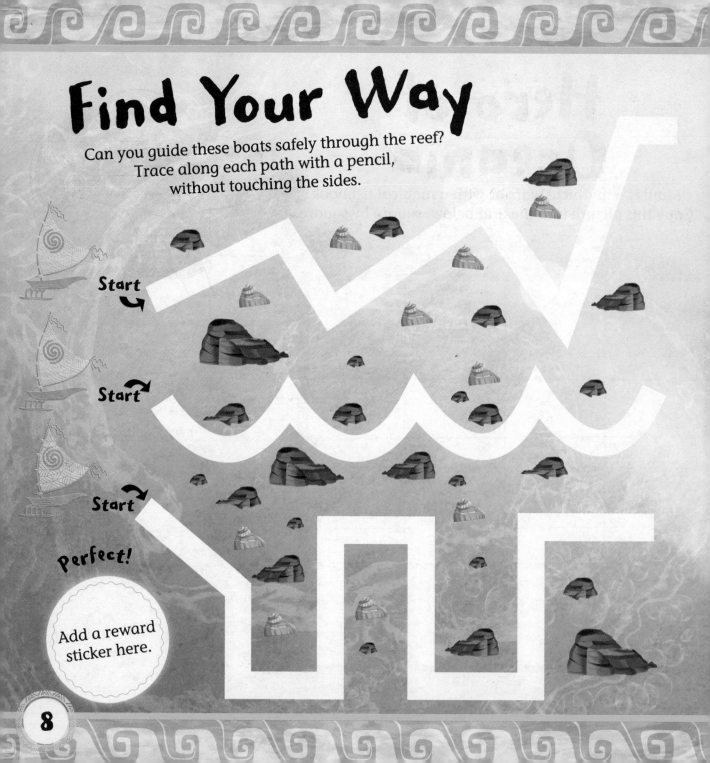

Start

Start

Start

Perfect!

Add a reward
sticker here.

Starry Sky

Moana can see a picture made out of stars in the sky.
Connect the numbered stars to reveal what it is.

You're a star!

Add a reward sticker here.

Answer on page 31

Matching Maui

Only one of the pictures below is exactly the same as the top picture of Maui. Can you find it?

a

b

c

d

e

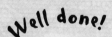

Add a reward sticker here.

10

Answer on page 31

Mythical Monster

What do you think lurks in the ocean beyond
Moana's island? Draw your own sea monster.

Great drawing!

Add a reward
sticker here.

Discover New Lands

Can you find Maui's island? It is the only island that is not part of a matching pair. Circle the correct island once you've found it.

a

b

c

d

Good job!

Add a reward sticker here.

e

Answer on page 31

Island Friends

Look at these pictures of Moana, Pua, and Heihei.
Can you circle the one that is different in each row?

1
a b c d

2
a b c d

3
a b c d

Did you spot them?

Add a reward sticker here.

13

Answers on page 31

Tapa Tracing

Trace over the design on Gramma Tala's Tapa cloth.
It shows Maui battling a giant octopus!
Now add color.

Fantastic!

Add a reward sticker here.

14

Magical Hook

Oh, no! Maui's fishhook is broken. Find the piece that matches the dotted outline and will complete the hook.

a

b

c

d

e

Great work!

Add a reward sticker here.

Pua the Pig

Poor Pua has lost his friend Moana.
Follow the shells to help him find her.

Finish

Start

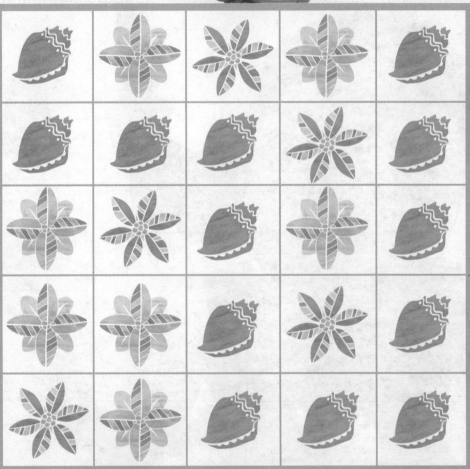

You did it!

Add a reward
sticker here.

16

Answer on page 31

Reward Stickers

© Disney

Just for Fun!

Shape-shifter

Maui can change himself into different animals.
Draw a line to match each animal to its name.
Then color in the pictures.

Bug ●

Lizard ●

Turtle ●

Hawk ●

Fish ●

Good work!

Add a reward
sticker here.

Island Explorers

Moana and Maui make a great team. Can you find five differences between these two pictures?

Good job!

Add a reward sticker here.

Color in a seashell for each difference you spot.

Answers on page 32

Mischief Makers

The Kakamora are little coconut-armored bandits.
Draw lines to link the matching pairs.

fantastic!

Add a reward
sticker here.

Top Rooster

Look at the top picture of Heihei.
Draw a circle around his matching shadow below.

a

b

d

c

Good work!

Add a reward sticker here.

Answer on page 32

Follow Your Heart

Guide Moana through the maze to reach the heart of Te Fiti, the island goddess.

Start here

Finish

You found it!

Add a reward sticker here.

Magical Maui

Maui has transformed into a hawk. Connect the dots to complete the picture, then add color before Maui flies away!

Start here ➤
1
2
3
4
5
6 7
8
9
10
11
12
13
14

Super!

Add a reward sticker here.

Ocean Explorers

Trace over the letters below to spell out the names of these Pacific island friends.

Moana

Maui

Heihei

Pua

Good writing!

Add a reward sticker here.

Island Paradise

Moana and her friends are having fun on the beach!
Tick each close-up when you find it in the big picture below.

Well done!

Add a reward sticker here.

Answers on page 31

Tropical Blooms

The island of Motunui is full of colorful flowers.
Decorate the flowers below.

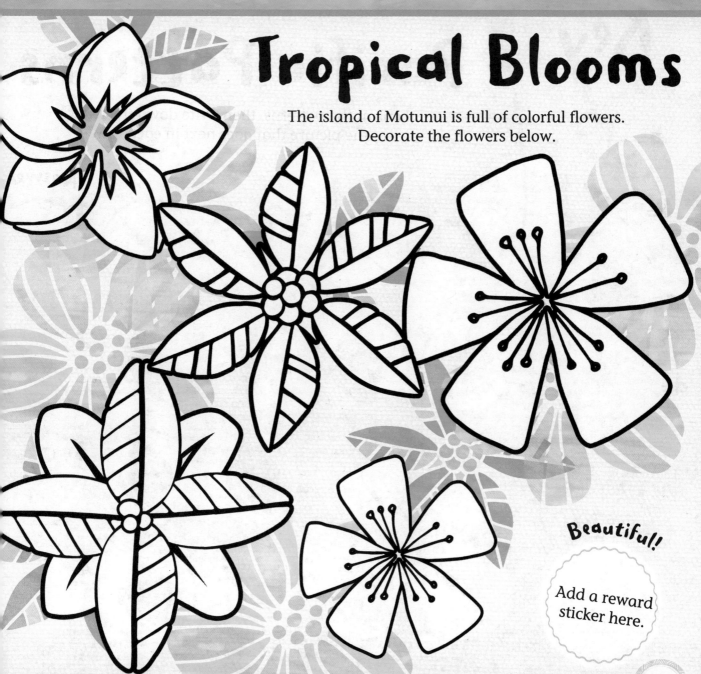

Beautiful!

Add a reward
sticker here.

Key

a =

b =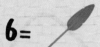

c =

d =

Pacific Patterns

Look at the patterns, then write down the letter
of the picture that goes next in each row.

Answers

1

2

3

4

Good job!

Add a reward
sticker here.

Answers on page 32

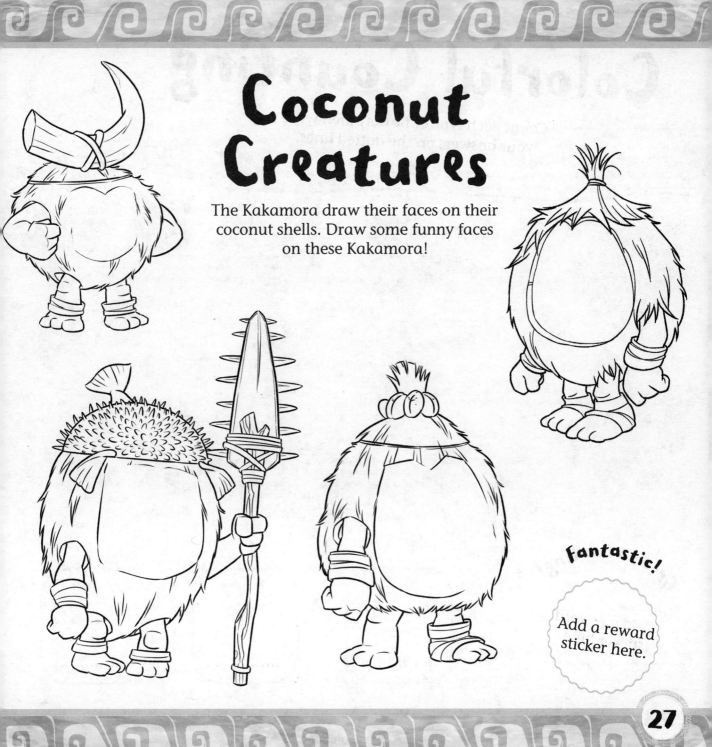

Coconut Creatures

The Kakamora draw their faces on their coconut shells. Draw some funny faces on these Kakamora!

Fantastic!

Add a reward sticker here.

27

Colorful Counting

Count each type of flower, then write
your answers on the dotted lines.

Great counting!

Add a reward
sticker here.

....

....

....

Answers on page 32

Oceanic Pals

How well do you know Moana and her friends?
Match each close-up to the correct character.

1
2
3
4

a

b

c

d

All matched up!

Add a reward
sticker here.

Island Daughter

Moana is giving little Pua a hug.
Color in these two best friends.

Beautiful coloring!

Add a reward
sticker here.

Answers

Page 2
There are seven shells.

Page 3
Path c leads to the ocean.

Page 5

'TUI' appears four times.

Page 9
Maui's fishhook.

Page 10
Picture d matches the top picture of Maui.

Page 12
Island d is Maui's island.

Page 13
1) b, 2) c, 3) a

Page 15
Piece e completes the hook.

Page 16

Page 17

 Turtle   Bug

 Lizard   Fish

 Hawk

Answers

Page 18

Page 24

Page 19

Page 20

Shadow b matches the picture of Heihei.

Page 21

Page 26

1) a, 2) d , 3) a, 4) b

Page 28

	4
	5
	6

Page 29

1) c, 2) a, 3) d, 4) b